STALKED BY THE RANCHER

EMMA BRAY

CHAPTER
ONE

Sawyer

I SWIPE the back of my hand across my forehead, the beads of sweat merging with the dust coating my skin. The sun's relentless rays beat down on the back of my neck as I stand in the middle of my kingdom—thousands of acres of land that stretch farther than the eye can see, all mine to command. The summer heat waves shimmer off the distant hills, and I squint against the glare.

"Hotter than a billy goat in a pepper patch," I mutter to myself, a wry grin tugging at my lips. My boots are planted firm in the dirt, worn leather scuffed from years of honest work. The cattle moo distantly, oblivious to the inferno bearing down on us.

I'm a man of the land, born and raised under this punishing Texas sun. My skin is permanently bronzed from years of laboring outdoors, the kind of tan that doesn't fade come winter. Muscles, honed from wrangling stubborn livestock and hefting hay bales, bunch and flex beneath my sweat-soaked shirt. Some guys hit the gym for this kind of build, but me? I just put in a hard day's work.

Pride swells in my chest like a hot air balloon. This ranch ain't just business. It's legacy, heritage. It's the Blackwood name etched into every fence post, whispered by every blade of grass. And as the latest Sawyer Blackwood to watch over these lands, I'll be damned if I don't pour every ounce of myself into it.

"Alright, time to saddle up," I tell myself, voice rough like gravel. "Let's get back to it." There's fences need mending, animals need feeding, and a hell of a lot more day left to conquer. With a last glance over my shoulder at the expanse I call home, I head toward the stables, ready for whatever comes next. Because that's what we Blackwoods do—we face the heat head-on and come out stronger for it.

———

I stride across the yard, boots kicking up dust that settles on my jeans like a second skin. The heat's relentless today, but I'm born and bred for this—built tough by years of sun and sweat.

"Damn," I mutter, pausing to lean on the fence, letting out a sigh that the dry wind snatches away. "Could sure use some company 'round here."

But the silence is my answer, and it gnaws at me, a hunger for connection that runs as deep as the wells on this land.

That's when I spot the dust cloud rolling down the long drive, a pickup truck barreling towards the ranch like it's got somewhere to be five minutes ago. My curiosity piques, and I straighten up, wiping more sweat from my brow as the vehicle comes to a halt near the main house.

"New help," I remind myself aloud, because hell, there's nobody else to remind.

The driver's door creaks open, and out steps Edward Davenport, his handshake as solid as his reputation. He's the new hired hand, come to give these old bones of mine a break from the day-to-day.

"Edward!" I call out, voice carrying over the hum of the idling engine. "Glad you could make it!"

"Wouldn't miss it for the world, Sawyer!" he replies, a grin splitting his weathered face.

And then, an angel steps out.

Holy fuck. Who is this?

She turns then, and our eyes lock. Got to be honest. I'm not ready for it. Not ready for the way her sun-kissed skin glows against the wild backdrop of my ranch, not ready for the way her hair spills around her shoulders like golden waves crashing on a sandy shore. She's got this lithe frame, see, one that speaks of youth but whispers promises of womanhood. It's an image that brands itself behind my eyelids, hot and unyielding.

"Sawyer, this is my daughter, Nora. Hope it's okay I brought her along."

Nora.

His fucking daughter.

I don't let my gaze linger—wouldn't be proper—but the image of her lingers in my mind like a brand. She's got this aura, like sunlight breaking through storm clouds, promising warmth after the chill.

"Welcome to Blackwood Ranch," I manage, schooling my features into a smile that's all professional, nothing personal. No sense in broadcasting my sudden interest. I've got a rep to protect.

But damn if this place doesn't feel a little less lonely already.

I watch her out of the corner of my eye.

Nora Davenport moves like she's got a secret melody playing just for her, a rhythm that's all sway and grace. She waltzes into my world, and hell if every dusty corner of this ranch doesn't brighten up. She's a breath of fresh air in the stifling summer heat, her youthful beauty hitting me square in the chest.

"Need a hand with that?" I call out, as I watch her pull a duffel bag from the truck bed, light as a feather despite its bulk.

"Got it, thanks!" Her voice is a melody too, and it dances over to me, settling under my skin. "But thank you, Mr. Blackwood." She smiles, and it's like the sun bursting through on a cloudy day.

"Call me Sawyer." I offer my hand, ignoring how rough and calloused it feels against the softness of hers.

"Okay...Sawyer." She says my name like it's something new, something exciting. And I can't help but want to hear it again and again.

"Let me show you around," I suggest, because standing here ain't doing any good to the pounding of my heart or the heat pooling low in my stomach.

As we walk, I steal glances at her when I think she won't notice. But who am I kidding? I'm about as subtle as a bull in a china shop. There's this pull, this goddamn magnetic force that's got my insides twisting up every time I look at her. I'm drawn to her, like I've been wandering in the dark and she's the first damn light I've seen in ages.

"Beautiful place you have here," Nora comments, her gaze sweeping over the acres of land.

"Thanks. It's my life's work." I puff up a bit, pride swelling in my chest as I watch her take it all in.

"Seems like a lot for one person," she observes, and there it is—she sees it, the loneliness I've got penned up inside.

"Sometimes it is," I admit, maybe too honestly.

"Well, maybe my dad and I can make it a little less so," she says, and the hope in her words is like a match to kindling.

"Maybe," I agree, voice rough with a desire I'm not supposed to feel.

Not this fast, not this fierce.

Not for a girl who looks like she's still in high school.

How old is she anyway?

Edward answers my unspoken question when he brags on his daughter, "Yeah, Nora's a senior in high school, and I thought getting some real-world experience would do her a world of good. She might only be eighteen, but she's a hard worker, my girl," he states proudly.

Eight-*fucking*-teen.

Goddamn it.

I feel like a pervert.

But then my eyes stray back over those long legs, that shapely ass, like a ripe little peach.

Fuuuck.

My breathing becomes ragged, and I feel my cock growing in my jeans.

Focus. The last thing I need is to be getting a hard-on for her right in front of her father.

I lead her and Edward through the stables, showing them where everything is and what I expect. Edward is very talkative, and I'm thankful to let him carry the conversation. The cat's got my tongue 'cause I can focus on is his daughter.

Every move she makes, every flutter of those long lashes, sends a jolt straight through me. It's like I'm a teen again, all hormones and heartbeats.

We finish the tour, and I'm already making plans to see her again, sooner rather than later. I'm consumed by her, by the idea of her—this young, beautiful creature who's stepped into my solitary world and turned it upside down. I want her, more than I've wanted anything in a long damn time.

———

I'm out in the fields, wrench in hand, when I see her again.

Nora.

She's hauling a bucket to the horses, and hell, that sight does things to me I can't even name. A voice in my head tells me to step back, cool down, but my feet have other plans. They're taking me straight to her.

"Need a hand with that?" I ask, voice rough like gravel, as I reach her side.

She looks up, all big green eyes and innocence. "I've got it, but thanks."

I take the bucket anyway, our fingers brushing, and damn if that touch doesn't shoot straight through me. I tell myself to play it cool.

"Strong hands," she comments, and I swear there's a hint of a tease in her tone.

"Comes with the job," I reply, trying for nonchalance. But inside, I'm a storm of wanting. It's like she's a magnet, and every cell in my body is iron filings, helpless to resist the pull.

We walk to the stable together, and I'm hyper-aware of her every move—the sway of her hips, the way her hair catches the sunlight. It should be illegal for someone to affect me this much.

"Bet you didn't think you'd be playing farmhand your senior year," I say, trying to steer my thoughts somewhere safer.

Her laugh is light and free, and it stirs something deep in my chest. "It's actually kind of exciting," she says. "Different from anything I've known."

"Good different, I hope." I set the bucket down and lean against the stall door, watching her.

"Definitely good," she replies, and there's that look again, like she's seeing right through me.

"Come on. Let me show you how to mix the feed properly," I find myself saying, another excuse to spend time with her. "It's all about getting the balance right."

She follows me, close enough that I can smell her—something sweet and floral that's probably from some shampoo, but it's intoxicating all the same. I talk her through the process, making sure our hands brush more than necessary.

"Like this?" she asks, holding up a scoop of feed for inspection.

"Exactly like that," I say, my voice dropping an octave. There's an energy between us now, a current that's impossible to ignore.

"Thanks, Sawyer. You're a good teacher," she says, and there's a warmth in her cheeks that matches the heat flooding my own body.

Fuck, if she only knew what I wanted to teach her.

"Anytime, Nora," I manage to choke out, already thinking about the next lesson I can give her. The next reason to be near her.

"See you later, then," she says, and heads off to finish her chores.

"Later," I echo, watching her go. And as she disappears from view, I press my hands hard against the wooden beams of the stable. I've got to keep a grip on this thing, on this wild desire that wants to consume me whole.

But even as I stand there, trying to steady myself, I know I'm kidding myself.

Because Nora Davenport isn't just under my skin.

She's in my blood, and I don't know how to want her any less.

———

The sun dips behind the horizon, and I'm alone in my room. The image of Nora, that lithe, vibrant thing, burns behind my eyelids. I lean back against the head-board, the sheets cool against my skin, but there's a fire raging inside me that's anything but.

Her laughter echoes in my ears—a sound I've caught myself chasing all damn day. And now, with the door closed and nothing but moonlight for company, I let my hand wander south. My breath hitches as I picture her, all soft curves and sun-kissed skin. In my mind, she's sprawled out beneath me, her body arching into mine. A low groan escapes me as I imagine her eyes, dark with desire, locked onto mine, and her sweet lips parted in a silent plea for more.

"Fuck, Nora," I rasp into the quiet, my movements

growing faster, rougher. I'm fucking my hand, bucking up into furiously, pretending it's her hot little cunt. I imagine she's hot and wet and tight. That my cock is the first one to breach her virginity.

And when release finally hits, it's like a goddamn thunderstorm breaking inside me. Her name is a reverent curse on my lips as I ride out the waves of pleasure, picturing her with me, around me, until there's nothing left but the echo of a fantasy and the reality of an empty room.

The next day, the heat clings to my skin, but it's got nothing on the burn in my chest when I catch sight of one of the ranch hands tossing Nora a flirty smile. She laughs, carefree and oblivious to the wildfire she's sparking in me.

"Hey!" I call out, my voice sharper than I intend. I stride over, slapping a heavy hand on the guy's shoulder. "Let's remember why we're here, yeah? This isn't a damn social hour."

"Easy, boss," he says, holding up his hands in surrender, and backs off. But my glare follows him like a shadow until he's well away from Nora. I turn to her, my jaw set, trying to smooth out the lines of possessiveness etched deep into my frown.

"Stick close to me today," I tell her, my voice low. "I've got some special tasks that need your attention."

"Special tasks?" she repeats, a flicker of confusion in

her eyes before she nods, unaware of the storm she's stirring up inside me.

"Very special," I affirm, watching the way the sunlight plays across her face, casting her in a glow that makes my chest tighten. "You'll see."

I don't miss the curious tilt of her head, nor the hesitant step she takes toward me. But it's clear as day—even if she doesn't understand it yet—that Nora Davenport is becoming my obsession. And I'll be damned if I let anyone else so much as think they've got a shot with her. She's *mine* to protect, *mine* to desire.

Mine to claim, whatever it takes.

———

I'm leaning against the fence, watching Nora as she moves with a grace that's got nothing to do with ranch work. Her every step is a siren call and I'm all too willing to crash on those rocks. She's bending over to pick up a saddle from the ground, and hell if my mind doesn't wander to less innocent bends and curves.

I've been coming up with bullshit tasks for her all day, things that I claim she needs me to show her how to do. All so I can come up with an excuse to be close to her.

Guard her from every other male who would look at her.

Mine.

We walk side by side to the stable, the air thick with everything unsaid. The horses seem to sense it too, their whinnies like a chorus to our silent song. I show her how to brush down old Betsy, our hands brushing more than once. Each contact sends a jolt through me, hot as the summer sun beating down on this Texas plain.

"Your dad's doing good work around here," I say, trying to sound casual, but really I'm fishing, wanting to know how much Edward Davenport's seen of what's simmering between his daughter and me.

"Thanks," she replies, her focus on Betsy's flank. "He likes it here. Says it's good to be busy."

"Keeps the mind off things," I add, thinking not for the first time how a busy mind is the last thing I want right now.

"Exactly," she agrees, unaware of the double entendre.

We walk side by side, Nora's lithe form keeping pace with my longer strides. I can feel the heat coming off her, even more intoxicating than the midday sun. Every now and then, I catch her sneaking looks at me, and it stokes the fire inside, makes me want to show her just how much of a man I am.

"See this here?" I stop and point to a loose wire on the fence, seizing the chance to press close as I feign fixing it. Our bodies touch, and it's electric, a current running straight through me.

"Looks like you've got strong hands," she says, bold and teasing, glancing up at me through those lashes.

"Strong enough to keep everything I care about safe," I murmur, locking eyes with her, letting her hear the promise in my voice.

She bites her lip, and my imagination runs away from me. I imagine how those lips would taste, how they would look wrapped around my cock…

The air between us crackles, charged with unspoken desires.

"Let's head back," I say after a moment, reluctant to end our time together but knowing there's a time for playing and a time for laying down your cards.

Nora nods, casting one last lingering glance at the horizon before we turn toward the house. The sun's dipping low, painting the sky in hues of fire and passion—fitting for the burn simmering under my skin.

Tonight, I'll lie awake, consumed with thoughts of her, imagining the taste of her lips, the feel of her soft curves beneath my calloused hands.

Because Nora Davenport is my obsession.

CHAPTER
TWO

Sawyer

I LEAN against the rough bark of an old oak, my gaze snagged on the scene before me. Nora's out there in the pasture, under the cruel kiss of the midday sun, her figure a silhouette against the blaze of the open sky. She bends over a stubborn weed, yanking it from the earth. Her movements are fluid, like she's part of the landscape—natural and wild.

Her skin's got that glow, you know? The kind that comes from days spent under the Texas sun, a rich caramel that makes my fingers twitch with the urge to touch. Nora's wearing these cutoffs that should be illegal, hugging every curve of her lithe frame in a way that has my blood heating up more than this damn heatwave.

She straightens, sweeping a loose strand of hair from her face, and even from this distance, I can see the sheen of sweat on her brow. It drips down, past her temple, teasing along the gentle curve of her neck. Jesus, what I wouldn't give to follow that trail with my lips, feel the beat of her pulse beneath my tongue.

She's like a mirage, all golden and glistening out there, making my throat dry. There's something about the way she moves, oblivious to the way she's got this grown man hiding behind trees just to steal a glimpse. A picture of innocence with a side of sin.

Nora pauses, tipping a water bottle to her lips, and I swear I can feel the cool rush down my own parched throat. She's a vision, all right—a siren call to a man who's been at sea for far too long. And hell if I'm not ready to crash against her rocks.

I bite the inside of my cheek, trying to rein in the wild stampede of desire that's been trampling through my mind since Nora stepped onto my land. It's a losing battle, and I know it. My gaze tracks her every move, latching onto the slightest sway of her hips as she bends to adjust an irrigation line.

"Get a grip, Sawyer," I mutter under my breath. But the reprimand falls flat even to my own ears. There's something about her, some magnetic pull that I can't seem to shake off. And damn if I haven't tried.

The heat isn't helping either. It wraps around me like a second skin, mirroring the heat that simmers low in my belly every time I picture those sun-kissed shoulders bare, free from the constraints of her tank top. My mouth goes dry at the thought, and it ain't just the summer drought causing it.

I imagine her laughter, light and airy, as I trace the outline of her collarbone with the tip of my finger, dipping lower to explore the valley between her breasts. The fantasy is vivid enough to make my hands shake. I see us tangled in the sheets of my bed, her body arched beneath mine, soft moans spilling from her lips as I—

"Jesus Christ." I scrub a hand down my face, feeling the day-old stubble scratch against my palm. This ain't right. She's young, innocent, and completely off-limits. I'm supposed to be looking after her, not undressing her with my eyes.

But hell, the heart wants what it wants—or maybe that's another part of me talking, the one that's been too long without a woman's touch. That voice whispers seduction in my ear, painting pictures of Nora splayed out on my desk, her legs wrapped around my waist as I bury myself inside her, claiming her over and over until all she can remember is my name.

"Shit." I press my knuckles to my lips, trying to stifle the groan that threatens to escape. I can almost feel her underneath me, her nails digging into my back, urging me on.

It's a dangerous game I'm playing, letting these fantasies take hold. They're a wildfire in my veins, and if I'm not careful, they'll burn us both alive. But for the life of me, I can't turn away—not when the mere idea of her, spread out and waiting for me, has me hard and aching with want.

"Control," I whisper to myself, a silent plea to whatever restraint I have left. It's a thin thread, fraying with each passing second I spend watching her from the shadows. I need to cool off, put some distance between us before I do something I'll regret.

"Tomorrow," I promise myself, the word tasting like ashes on my tongue. "I'll stay away tomorrow."

But even as I say it, I know it's a lie. Tomorrow, I'll be right back here, caught in the gravitational pull of Nora's orbit, helpless against the tide of desire that's threatening to sweep me under.

I slam the door to my study behind me, breathing hard. The heat of the day clings to my skin, but it's nothing compared to the fire raging inside me. My hands are shaking as I lock the door, a flimsy barrier between the world and my shameful secret.

"Get a grip," I mutter to myself, even as I stride across the room to the bottom drawer of my desk. It's a little corner of hell that I've carved out for myself, filled with stolen moments captured in still frames.

My fingers curl around the stack of photos hidden there—the weight of them both a comfort and a condemnation. Each snapshot is a glimpse into a life I can't have, shouldn't even want. But God, how I want it.

Nora's face smiles up at me from the glossy paper, her eyes sparkling with laughter in one, her brow furrowed in concentration in another. She's blissfully unaware of the camera, of my gaze forever etched onto these moments. My chest tightens as I thumb through them, the images blurring as anticipation coils tight in my belly.

"Damn," I groan, my voice low and rough. The pictures spread out before me fan the flames of desire until it's all-consuming, devouring every shred of decency I pretend to have.

I sit heavily in my chair, the leather creaking under my weight. The image of Nora bent over a fence post, sunlight painting her curves in a golden hue, has me gripping the edge of the desk. I'm panting now, heart thundering like a stallion's hooves against the ground, each beat echoing my need, my craving for release.

"Shit, I'm in deep," I confess to the silent room, to the walls that hold my secrets. Sweat beads on my forehead as I fight the gnawing guilt, the part of me that knows this isn't right. But the raw hunger drowns out the voice of reason, leaving only the primal urge to claim, to possess.

"Fuck control," I hiss, giving in to the darkness that's been hounding my steps, stalking me like a predator. Every cell in my body screams for relief, and I'm too damn weak to deny it any longer.

I tear my gaze from the images scattered across the desk and focus on one in particular—Nora, her hair a wild mane framing her face, cheeks flushed with exertion. Her lips are parted, as if calling out to me, begging for something only I can give. My hand moves to my belt, unbuckling it with practiced ease.

"God, Nora," I groan, my voice a mere whisper as I free myself from the confines of denim. The cool air hits my heated skin, contrasting with the heat that's pooling in my groin. I wrap my fingers around myself, my grip firm, just like I imagine hers would be. The fantasy sends a jolt straight through me.

"Would you touch me like this?" I mutter, thumbing through the pictures with my other hand. Each image is another note in the symphony of my desire, every curve and shadow a melody that drives me closer to the edge.

My movements are rough, needy, as I stroke myself in time with the visions dancing in my head—Nora beneath me, her body arching into mine, those sun-kissed legs wrapped tight around my waist. I picture her whispers, her moans, all for me, as I take her in the soft hay of the barn loft, where the scent of earth and desire mingle in the heavy air.

"Damn, girl, you're gonna be the death of me," I rasp. My strokes become more erratic, faster, as I chase the pleasure that threatens to consume me whole. I'm close, so damn close, riding the razor's edge between control and utter abandon.

"Ah, fuck," I grunt as I feel the pressure build, a crescendo of need that has no outlet but this. The thought of her soft curves yielding under my hands, her gasps and cries filling the room, it's all too much. I'm teetering on the brink, sweat slicking my skin as I barrel toward release.

And then, it crashes over me—a wave of ecstasy so powerful it whites out my vision. "Nora!" Her name bursts from me, a raw shout that echoes off the walls of my study. Pleasure racks my body, my muscles clenching and unclenching, as I spill myself with a shudder of satisfaction that leaves me breathless.

For a moment, there's nothing but the sound of my

ragged breathing and the soft crackle of paper under my hand. The tension that's been winding tighter all day snaps, leaving me drained but sated, the relentless craving momentarily quelled. I lean back in my chair, letting the afterglow wash over me, basking in the silence that follows the storm.

My panting slows, though my heart is still a wild drum in my chest. I'm coming down from that high, the rush of release ebbing away, and fuck, it leaves room for something else to seep in—guilt. It coils around me, heavy and tight, squeezing until I can barely think.

"Shit," I mutter to myself, my voice a rough whisper in the quiet room. The pictures of Nora are scattered on my desk, her eyes staring back at me from each one. They're innocent snapshots, but I've tainted them, turned them into fuel for my own burning desires. My gut twists because she doesn't know. She can't know how far I've gone.

I swipe a hand over my face, feeling the sticky residue of sweat and self-loathing. Gaze dropping to the photos, each one is a reminder of the line I've crossed. Nora, with her sun-kissed skin and smile that could light up the darkest places in me, deserves better than to be an object in my twisted fantasy.

"Get your shit together, Blackwood," I scold myself, the sound of my full name a slap to pull me out of this spiral. I gather the pictures, my hands careful not to crumple them, not after what they've just been through. Each image is a confession of my obsession, and as I stack them neatly, I can't help feeling like I'm trying to put my soul back in order.

With every picture I slip back into the hidden compartment in my desk, there's a promise to myself. Be the man she thinks you are, not this...not this guy who gets off to stolen moments.

"Control," I breathe out, the word a mantra. It has to mean something again. Control over the ranch, control over my damn self.

Photos tucked away, I lock the compartment with a decisive click. It's done. The evidence of my shame secured once more, where it can't hurt anyone but me.

Nora

"HAND ME THAT HAMMER, would you, Nora?" Sawyer's voice rolls over the field like distant thunder, casual yet somehow commanding. I'm squatting beside a pile of weathered wood planks and rusted nails, trying to appear more useful than I feel.

"Uh, sure," I say, fumbling with the heavy tool before passing it to him. My hands are already blistered, my experience limited to the theoretical knowledge from YouTube tutorials I crammed last night.

"Never taken a swing at a fence post before, huh?" He doesn't look up from where he's steadying a post, but his teasing tone is as clear as the blue Texas sky above us.

"Does it show that much?" I ask, attempting to match his playful banter.

"Only a little." Sawyer shoots me a wink, his sun-kissed arm muscles flexing as he positions the new section of the fence. "You're doing fine. Just watch and learn."

"From the master, right?" I quip back, earning a grin that could probably outshine the sun.

"Exactly. Don't worry. I'll make a ranch hand out of you yet," he chuckles, sending a warm ripple through me.

It's funny. He hired my dad, but he's spent more time training me than Dad.

Of course, it's my own fault. I know that. I saw him the other day and offered to help him with some things. But what girl could blame me? The man is the definition if h-o-t, and I don't know. I just want to be around him.

I try to focus on handing him the tools he needs, but it's hard not to get distracted by the way his shirt stretches across his back, outlining every move he makes. The fence might as well be a million miles away for all the attention I can muster.

"Here, hold this steady for me," Sawyer instructs, motioning for me to come closer.

Our bodies align as I press against the wooden rail to stabilize it. And that's when it happens—Sawyer reaches past me, his rough fingers grazing my forearm. Was it intentional?

A spark of electricity zips through my body, lighting up paths I didn't even know existed. I swallow hard, trying to maintain some semblance of composure.

"Oops, sorry about that," he murmurs. His eyes lock onto mine, and I watch his Adam's apple bob as he swallows.

"Fine, it's...no problem," I stammer, feeling the heat rising in my cheeks.

"Good to know," he replies softly, his voice dropping an octave. There's a charged silence, filled only by our breathing and the distant call of a hawk overhead.

The tension between us thickens, the air practically vibrating with unsaid words and unexplored possibilities. Every casual touch sends a jolt through me, awakening a longing that I've never allowed myself to fully acknowledge.

"Looks like we're making progress," Sawyer finally says, breaking the moment as he steps back to admire our handiwork.

"Thanks to the teacher," I manage to say, throwing in a smile to cover up the turmoil inside.

"Anytime, Nora," he says, his gaze lingering a bit too long to be purely professional.

As we continue working side by side, his teasing remarks take on a new edge, each word laced with an undercurrent of something wild and untamed.

And I can't help but wonder what it would be like to let that current sweep me away.

———

The sun beats down, fierce and relentless, as Sawyer wipes his brow with the back of his hand. He catches me eyeing the shimmering creek beyond the fence line and grins.

"Whatcha say we take a break, Nora? That water's callin' our names." His voice is smooth, like gravel washed over by a gentle stream.

"Are you serious?" I ask, my eyes widening at the thought of the cool water against my skin.

"Never been more serious in my life." He starts toward the creek, unbuttoning his shirt as he goes.

I follow, my heart racing. The idea of swimming with Sawyer sends a thrilling shiver down my spine. We reach the bank, and I watch, almost in a trance, as he peels off his shirt, revealing a chest that's all hard planes and taut muscle. He dives in, splashing up a crystal spray, and beckons me with a devilish smirk.

"Come on in, the water's perfect!"

I hesitate only for a second before kicking off my boots and pulling off my shirt and jeans, revealing the plain bra and panties I wear underneath. I tell myself that it's no different from wearing a bikini.

His gaze sweeps over me, lingering just long enough to ignite a fire deep in my belly.

The cold rush of water envelopes me as I plunge in, and a gasp escapes my lips. Sawyer is beside me in an instant, his hands finding my waist as he steadies me. Our laughter mingles, echoing off the surrounding trees, as we splash each other playfully, the rest of the world melting away.

"Gotcha!" I squeal, sending a wave of water his way.

"Is that how it's gonna be?" he challenges, his eyes flashing with mischief.

"Maybe," I tease, trying to swim away, but he's quick, capturing me in a gentle but firm grip.

"Caught ya," he whispers, and for a moment we're just there, floating, the tension between us as palpable as the droplets on our skin.

Eventually, we clamber out onto the bank, breathless and dripping. As I wring out my hair, Sawyer's already digging through his backpack.

"Here, put this on," he says, offering me his shirt. "Gotta protect that soft skin of yours from the sun."

"Thanks," I murmur, taking the fabric from him. It's warm from his body, smelling faintly of sweat and something uniquely Sawyer.

"Need help?" he asks, a hint of huskiness in his voice.

"Sure," I reply, my breath hitching.

He steps behind me, and as he helps guide my arms through the sleeves, his fingers brush lightly against my bare skin, sending ripples of desire cascading through me. I tilt my head back slightly, catching his eye.

"Perfect fit," he murmurs, his hands resting on my shoulders a moment longer than necessary.

"Feels like you're still holding me," I whisper, turning to face him.

"Wouldn't be the worst thing," he says, his voice low as his gaze drifts to my lips.

"Definitely not the worst," I agree, my heart thundering against my ribcage, aware of the growing heat between us even as the shirt hangs loose and open around my frame.

"Better button up," he suggests, though his hands make no move to leave me.

"Maybe in a minute," I reply, realizing that with every word, every touch, I'm coming undone under the spell of Sawyer Blackwood.

He finally steps back and clears his throat. "What

do you say we grab a bite to eat? My treat for working you so hard today?"

All I can do is nod.

———

I slide into the booth across from Sawyer, the worn red leather creaking under me. The diner is a cozy, neon-lit slice of Americana with the scent of fried food lingering in the air like a savory promise.

"Thanks for inviting me," I say, picking up the laminated menu. It's sticky and has probably seen better days, but it feels warm, familiar.

"Least I can do after you slaved away fixing fences with me," he says, his eyes crinkling at the corners. "Besides, I heard how much you love pie, and they have the best pie in the world hear."

"Guilty as charged." I grin. "But if we're talking about hard work, you're the one who should be getting the royal treatment."

"Watching you handle those tools today? That was my treat." His voice is playful, but there's a heat to it that makes my cheeks flush.

"Careful now, don't make me think you enjoyed the view more than my stellar handiwork." I tease, but inside, my stomach flutters like a field full of butterflies taking flight.

"Can't it be both?" He leans forward, forearms resting on the table, bringing his face closer to mine.

"Maybe," I concede, allowing the word to linger between us, heavy with possibility.

The waitress comes over and we order, exchanging smiles and small talk until she leaves. Then, it's back to the dance of our conversation—flirtatious, charged. With every word, I feel myself being pulled deeper into whatever this thing is with Sawyer Blackwood.

"Enjoy your chicken fried steak," the waitress says as our meals arrive, "and don't forget to save room for dessert."

"Sweetheart, I always have room for dessert," Sawyer replies, but he's not looking at the waitress. His gaze is heavy on me and burning with something intense—something I can't even identify.

"Good to know," I murmur, my heart pounding in sync with the jukebox's rhythm.

After dinner, he insists on paying, brushing off my protests with a wave of his hand. "This is just part one of tonight's thank-you," he says, leading me outside.

"Part two?" I ask, curious and a little breathless as we step out into the cool night.

"Yep. Follow me." He heads towards his truck, and I trail behind him, the gravel crunching beneath our boots.

We climb into his truck, the interior smelling like

leather and something distinctly masculine. I shiver as he starts the engine, the rumble vibrating through the seat and into my bones.

"Where to?" I ask, as we pull away from the diner.

"Somewhere quieter," Sawyer says, casting me a sidelong glance that sends a rush of heat swirling in my belly.

"Quieter than this?"

"Trust me," he murmurs, and I realize that I do. Implicitly.

The drive is silent except for the sound of tires on the road and the occasional hum of the engine. His hand rests casually on the gearshift, inches from my thigh. I'm hyperaware of the space between us, of the warmth emanating from his body, of the charged air that seems to crackle with electricity.

"Look at that sky," he says, after what feels like an eternity or maybe just a moment. He pulls off onto a dirt road, the truck bouncing slightly as we head into the open landscape.

Stars pepper the black canvas above us, so bright and numerous they look like they've been sprinkled by a divine hand. We're moving away from the rest of the world, into a place that feels like it belongs only to us.

"Beautiful," I whisper, not sure if I'm talking about the stars or the man next to me.

"Nothing compared to you, darlin'," he replies, his voice low and rough.

I turn to look at him and find his gaze already on me. There's a promise in his eyes, a silent vow that sends another shiver down my spine.

"Stop it," I say, but it's half-hearted, and we both know it.

"Stop what?" He feigns innocence, but the corner of his mouth quirks up in a knowing smile.

"Making me feel like...like..."

"Like you're the only person in the world?" he finishes for me, pulling the truck to a stop.

"Exactly like that," I confess, my pulse racing.

The truck rolls to a stop, and the world outside is a still painting of moonlight on sagebrush and rock. Sawyer kills the engine and the silence rushes in, as vast as the desert stretching out around us.

"Come on," he says with that half-grin that's all trouble, and I'm unbuckling before my brain catches up with his intent.

We're stepping into the cool night air, the kind of quiet where you can almost hear the stars twinkling if you listen hard enough. He grabs my hand, leading me to a spot where the earth dips and the sky opens wide.

"Wow," slips from me because there's no other word for it. The heavens are spread above us like a dark velvet sheet dotted with endless diamonds, and I'm caught, breathless.

"Beautiful, isn't it?" Sawyer's voice is low beside me, sending ripples across my skin.

Before I can respond, he's pulling me close, his arms wrapping around me in a move as smooth as the slide of silk. Our bodies press together, and I can feel every line of his muscular frame against mine. His heat seeps into me and I'm melting, melting...

"Look up," he whispers, and I tilt my head back against his shoulder, gazing up at the cosmic dance above. His chest rises and falls against my back, and I'm caught in the rhythmic tide of his breathing.

"Ever seen anything like it?" he asks, his lips brushing the shell of my ear, and I shiver.

"Never." The word is barely a breath, but it's true. The stars have nothing on the man holding me.

"I imagine this right here is why my grandparents chose this place to build," Sawyer admits softly.

I don't speak, sensing he's going to say more.

"They built the ranch with their bare hands," Sawyer explains, pride lacing his words. "And every generation has added to it."

"Tell me their story," I urge, hungry for more than just the history.

As he recounts tales of love, hardship, and triumphs, I see a new layer to Sawyer Blackwood—a man deeply rooted in legacy, yet standing right here with me, vulnerable and open. Each word is a window into his world, and as he shares them, it's like he's giving me pieces of his soul.

"Your turn," he says after a while, eyes searching mine.

"Me?" My life seems small compared to the epic saga he just told me.

"Everyone's got a story, Nora. What's yours?"

"Nothing special," I demur, but Sawyer shakes his head.

"Come on, darlin'. Surprise me."

So, I start with the little things—my favorite books, the summer I learned to swim, the scar on my knee from a bike accident. And Sawyer listens, really listens, his gaze never leaving mine. In this quiet night, filled with the echoes of the past, we're weaving a new narrative, one that's just ours.

We talk until I don't know what time it is, and I realize this is no longer just about flirtation or games.

This is something real, something that could last longer than a summer on the ranch.

"Thank you," I whisper, touched by the trust he's shown in sharing his family's legacy with me.

"Thank you," he replies, his hand finding mine across the table, warm and certain. "For listening."

I look up at him, and there it is.

That look he gives me, that super intense look that makes my heart want to skip a beat.

His lips part, and am I imagining it, or is his head moving closer to mine?

A thousand thoughts run through my mind.

Yes, I want this. I want him to kiss me.

But he's my boss. He's so much older than me. He technically hired my dad. Could this get my dad fired?

But then it all fades away when Sawyer's lips finally touch mine.

My eyes slip closed and fireworks explode behind my eyelids.

Sawyer's lips are firm yet gentle, coaxing mine open with a practiced finesse that leaves me reeling. His tongue dances with mine, tasting of cinnamon and something quintessentially *him*.

I melt into him, my body aching for more of this contact, this connection. His hands roam down my sides, leaving a trail of fire everywhere they touch.

Wetness pools between my thighs, and I whimper into his mouth.

"Fuck," Sawyer murmurs before he pulls me tight against him, "Do you know what you do to me, little girl?"

Before I can answer, he captures my lips again, his tongue swooping back into my mouth to kiss me more deeply this time.

I can taste the want in his kiss, the desire burning like a sun going supernova. His hands move from my sides to my lower back, pulling me closer till we're as pressed together as two bodies can be without becoming one.

His fingers dig into my flesh through my shirt, and I can't help but arch into him, inviting him to touch me more. I whimper when he takes the invitation, his hand slipping beneath my shirt to make contact with bare skin.

His calloused palm is warm against the small of my back and I shudder, half because it feels so damn good and half because it's Sawyer...Sawyer Blackwood, doing this to me.

"Is this...okay?" he rasps out between kisses, pulling back just enough to look into my eyes. His pupils are blown wide with desire and I know mine must mirror his own.

"Yes," I gasp out, "Yes, it's beyond okay."

He smiles then, a wolfish grin that has me thinking of wild, untamed nights under these very stars. He crushes our lips together once again and I let myself go further into him.

His hands start moving lower now, tracing the curve of my hips before gripping my thighs. He lifts me up as if I weigh nothing and I instinctively wrap my legs around his waist.

My skirt rides up dangerously high from the movement and I can feel his hard length against me even through our clothes. It makes me heady with desire, knowing that I'm the one who did this to him.

"You're shaking," he whispers against my lips and indeed I am—not out of fear, but anticipation. His words are sandpaper against my heated skin, and I crave more.

"I...I..."

But he silences me with a kiss, his lips moving over mine, frying every thought in my brain. His hands explore my body in ways I've only ever dreamed of, lighting up nerve endings I didn't know existed.

"What do you want, Nora?" He breathes into my ear, his voice husky with desire.

"You," I admit, my voice barely above a whisper. It feels like the biggest secret I've ever told. But it's not a secret at all. it's the truth. A truth I can no longer ignore or hide from.

Sawyer doesn't say anything for a moment, just holds me tighter. Then he lets out a low growl that sends shivers down my spine and grinds his hips against mine—a crude but oh-so-enticing movement that has me gasping aloud.

"I've wanted to hear you say that from the moment I laid eyes on you," he admits hoarsely.

My heart flutters at this admission.

His mouth descends on mine again and the conversation ends there—replaced with moans and gasps and whispered promises between shared breaths. His hands are everywhere, claiming what's his—marking me as his own.

He slips my clothes from my body until I'm standing naked before him, and then he stands there and stares at me slack-jawed.

"More beautiful than I even fucking imagined," he rasps out as he grips his cock roughly through his pants. "Fuck, I could come just looking at you, baby."

My heart races at his admission, and then the next thing I know, I'm in his arms again.

His lips press against mine with a fervor that sends shivers down my spine and liquid heat pooling between my thighs. His hands are everywhere, kneading my breasts, squeezing my ass, sliding over every inch of me like he's trying to memorize the feel of my naked body against his.

"God, Nora," he pants into my ear, "I've never wanted anyone like I want you."

The words send a thrill through me. I arch into him, whimpering when his lips close around a nipple. His hand slides down my belly, inching closer and closer to the aching space between my thighs. My hips buck against him as I plead for more.

"Please," I whisper, my fingers tangling in his hair

as he lavishes attention on my breasts. "I need...I need..."

"Shhh, darlin'," he murmurs against my skin, his voice thick with lust. "I know what you need."

Then his fingers are there, parting my folds and dipping inside me. I gasp loudly at the sensation, reeling from the intimate touch.

"You're so fucking wet for me." He growls.

His fingers move expertly, stroking and teasing and creating a storm of pleasure that has me crying out. My hips roll into his touch, seeking more, always more.

"Fuck, baby," he groans, "You like that?"

"Yes," I pant, "Don't stop."

I hear his chuckle just before he dips his head to replace his fingers with his tongue. The sensation is almost too much and I grab onto his hair as if it's my only lifeline. His lips and tongue work magic, pulling moans and cries from me till I'm shaking with the intensity of it all.

Sawyer brings me to the edge, then backs off just enough to keep me hovering there—a quivering mess under the open sky.

"You're fucking beautiful when you come apart for me," he rasps against my skin. "I want to see your face when I fill you up for the first time."

Roughly, he pulls me back into a standing position, spinning me around till my naked body is pressed against the rough bark of a tree. I gasp, both in surprise and anticipation.

His strong arm wraps around my waist, pulling me flush against him. His hard cock presses against my ass through the fabric of his jeans. He grinds against me in slow circles, making me writhe and whimper for more.

"I want you now," he growls in my ear, "Tell me you want it too."

"Yes… oh yes…" I moan out.

He hastily unzips his jeans freeing his substantial length. A moment later, he slides inside me slowly.

I cry out at the delicious stretch of him, my body seeking to accommodate his size. Every inch of him fills me, burning and perfect.

His hands grip my waist, his movements unhurried as he slides in and out. His breath is ragged as he buries himself within me again and again.

"My Nora," he rasps in my ear, "So tight...so perfect...*mine*."

I can only whimper in response, lost in the sensation of him moving within me. The world narrows down to just us, just this moment. His cock thrusting into me, our bodies joined.

I'm close again, so fucking close I can taste it. I whimper, grinding back against him and he groans deep in his chest, thrusting harder.

With a final cry, I come apart around him and

Sawyer follows a moment later. He buries his face into the crook of my neck as he empties himself inside me. Our gasps and panting fill the silence that follows.

"I...I didn't know it could feel like this," I admit when I finally find my voice.

He chuckles against my skin, sending shivers down my spine. "Believe me, darlin'. This is just the beginning." He promises with another roll of his hips that has me gasping again.

And just like that, under the stars with Sawyer Blackwood – rugged rancher and my boss – I lose myself.

"You're mine now," Sawyer whispers against my lips before he plants another branding kiss on my lips again.

CHAPTER
FOUR

Sawyer

I LEAN against the wooden fence, watching Nora laugh across the field, her hair catching the late afternoon sun like strands of gold. My chest tightens, a mix of pride and something darker, something hungry. She's *mine*, and I intend to keep it that way.

"Hey, Sawyer!" Tommy Jenkins' voice cuts through my thoughts like a dull blade, and I straighten up, fixing him with a look that's chilled more than one man to the bone.

"Tommy," I say, my voice low and even. "What can I do for you?"

He shuffles his feet, looking all of eighteen and too

damn young to be messing with fire. I follow his gaze, and my jaw tightens. I've seen the way he's been looking at Nora. I don't give a fuck if he is one of my best ranch hands. "Man, that Nora..."

There it is. The spark. It lights the fuse in me, jealousy coiling like barbed wire around my gut. All I can think about is wiping her name off his lips. I step closer, close enough for him to see the warning in my eyes, feel the threat rolling off me in waves.

"Listen here, boy," I growl, my words deliberate and heavy with intent. "Nora's not the kind of girl you take out on some high school date. She's...special."

Tommy swallows hard, his Adam's apple bobbing like a buoy at sea. "Sawyer, I didn't mean—"

"Save it," I cut him off, my glare unrelenting. "Stay away from her, Tommy. This isn't a request."

He nods, taking a step back, and I know I've made my point clear. He'll spread the word. Sawyer Blackwood's got his sights set on Nora Davenport, and there's not a damn thing anyone can do about it.

I watch him retreat, and unclench fists I didn't even realize I'd made.

"Blackwood!" The voice behind me is like gravel, rough and grinding.

Edward Davenport, Nora's father.

Shit-fire.

"Edward," I reply without turning, already knowing

this conversation is going to be as pleasant as a rattlesnake bite.

"You think I don't see what's going on?" Edward states, his tone accusing as he steps into my line of sight, brows furrowed with concern and something fiercer. "You're a grown man, Sawyer. What the hell are you doing with my daughter?"

"Easy, Edward," I say, my voice calm but my insides churning. "You're reading it wrong."

"Am I?" He's practically spitting the words. "She's a kid, Sawyer. And you're filling her head with ideas, showering her with attention. Don't think I haven't noticed."

"Your daughter isn't a child," I say firmly, meeting his gaze without flinching. "She's a woman, and she knows her own mind."

"Knows her own mind?" His laugh is bitter. "You're twice her age, and you've got experience she can't even imagine. You could be using that, taking advantage..."

"Hey now," I interject, feeling a flare of anger at the accusation. "I respect Nora. Everything between us is mutual, believe me."

"Mutual," he repeats, skepticism written all over his face. "I don't care if you are my boss, Blackwood. If you hurt her—"

"You won't have to worry about that," I assure him,

but the edge in my voice makes it sound more like a threat than a promise.

Edward shakes his head, muttering under his breath as he stalks away. I watch him go, the weight of his words settling on my shoulders like a winter coat. But it doesn't change anything.

Nora's under my skin, in my blood, and I'll do whatever it takes to make sure she stays mine.

The sun dips lower, casting long shadows on the ground, and I turn back to the fields. Tonight, Nora will be with me, and I'll show her pleasures that will make her forget boys like Tommy ever existed. Because when it comes to Nora, I'm playing for keeps.

———

Nora

I'm leaning against the hood of Sawyer's glossy black truck, the cool metal barely registering against my thighs through the thin fabric of my dress. The night sky is a blanket of stars, each one twinkling like a promise of something more—something wild and uncharted. I can't help but feel caught between two worlds: the one where I'm Daddy's little girl, and the one where I'm the object of Sawyer Blackwood's burning desire.

"Beautiful, isn't it?" Sawyer's voice rumbles from behind me, warm breath tickling my ear. He's close, too close, his body heat enveloping me in a way that makes my insides twist with a delicious tension.

"Yeah," I whisper back, my gaze still fixed on the heavens above. "It's like nothing I've ever seen before."

"You're like nothing I've even seen before," he says as he wraps an arm around my waist, pulling me back against his solid chest, and I can feel that all-too-familiar thrill coursing through me. His touch is possessive, sure, but it's also protective in a way that has my heart racing.

"I missed you today," I admit, letting myself rest against him for just a moment longer before stepping away. There's a part of me that's screaming to stay right there, wrapped up in his strength. But then there's another, quieter voice reminding me of the looks Dad's been giving us—the suspicion in his eyes.

"Come here, darlin'," Sawyer says, and before I know it, he's sweeping me into his arms and walking towards the front porch. He sets me down gently on the top step and crouches in front of me. From his pocket, he pulls out a small velvet box and opens it to reveal a shimmering necklace, the diamonds catching the moonlight and throwing sparks into the darkness.

"Jesus, Sawyer...I can't..." The protest dies on my lips as he fastens the necklace around my throat, his fingers brushing my skin in a way that sends shivers down my spine.

"Can't what? Accept a gift from someone who cares about you?" His blue eyes are intense, drilling into mine with an emotion I can't quite name. It's more than lust. It's almost like a plea.

"Isn't it too much?" I ask, my voice barely a whisper.

"Nothing's too much for you, Nora." He stands, towering over me, and there's that edge of possessiveness again. "I want you to have everything. Anything you want, it's yours."

And damn if that doesn't make me feel like the most important girl in the world. I want to tell him that he doesn't need to buy me pretty things—that his smile, his touch, the way he looks at me like I'm the only woman on earth is more than enough.

But then he's kissing me, hard and deep, and I'm lost in the taste of him, the feel of his body pressed against mine. It's passionate and raw, and I can't bring myself to pull away, not even when the rational part of my brain is reminding me that we should be careful. That my dad might see.

The truth is, Sawyer Blackwood has become the most addictive thing in my world, and as we stumble inside, hands roaming and lips locked, I can't find it in me to care about anything else.

I know I'm playing with fire, but God, if this isn't the hottest, most exhilarating burn I've ever felt.

And suddenly I want to try something. I want to make Sawyer feel how good he makes me feel.

So, I drop to my knees in front of him and look up at him shyly as I start to unbuckle his belt.

His breath hitches as he watches me.

"S-Sweetheart," he stammers, his big, calloused hands reaching out to stop me. But I swat them away, my fingers fumbling for a moment as I push past his initial resistance.

It's my first time doing anything like this, but there's a fire inside me, an urgency that drowns out any uncertainty. I can't ignore the way his breath catches in his throat when I touch him, or the way his body responds to my every move. It emboldens me, reassures me that I'm not alone in this.

"Relax, cowboy," I say teasingly, looking up at him through my lashes as I work at the button on his jeans. His eyes never leave mine. They're dark and filled with something intense—a mixture of desire and...vulnerability?

"Nora," he says roughly, his hands tangling in my hair as he lets out a breathless laugh. "You're gonna be the death of me."

But he doesn't stop me. In fact, he leans back against the wall, watching me with a kind of awe that sends shivers down my spine.

I want to explore him, to learn every curve and angle of his body until I know it as well as my own.

There's a bead of moisture on the swollen tip of his cock nad I lick it gently. His taste is intoxicating—a tantalizing blend of masculinity and sweat that leeches into my skin and leaves me wanting more.

His hands fist in my hair, and there's a thump as his head falls back against the wall as I slide him all the way into my mouth—taking as much of him inside as I can. I feel the head of his cock hit the back of my throat, and I still don't have him all the way inside my mouth.

"Nora..." His voice is trembling, his body rigid as he tries to control himself. It's intoxicating, knowing I have this kind of power over a man like Sawyer Blackwood. He may be older, more experienced, but right now, he's at my mercy.

I'm not sure I'm doing it right—hell, I've only ever seen this in movies—but he seems to be enjoying it. His grip on my hair tightens as I begin moving my head, the pull of his hands guiding me. The sensation is overwhelming—the taste of him, the feel of him pulsing against my tongue, and the throaty groans that escape him.

"Fuck… darlin'…" Sawyer swears under his breath,

hips bucking involuntarily. He's fighting for control, his knuckles white where they're gripping my hair. A part of me swells with pride. I'm doing this– driving Sawyer Blackwood to the brink with just my mouth.

But then he's pulling me back gently, a string of curses tumbling from his lips as he gazes down at me with hooded eyes.

"No more, darling," he pants out. "If you keep going… God."

I blink up at him innocently, licking my lips clean. Just the sight of him—flustered and breathless because of me—it sends a thrill through me.

"I wanted to make you feel good," I say softly.

He laughs breathlessly at that and hauls me up against him. "Oh sweetheart," he murmurs against my lips. "You did. More than good."

We stumble back towards his bedroom then—me giggling and him grinning like a madman, both of us high on the taste of the other. His hands roam over me as he paws at my clothing, stripping me down with a primal need that leaves me breathless.

"You're beautiful," he whispers against my skin, his lips trailing a path down my neck and over my chest. The touch of his hands and mouth against my bare skin sends sparks of pleasure radiating through me.

He diverts to the side, tracing the line of diamonds hugging my neck, his eyes never leaving mine. "Perfect," he murmurs, fingers ghosting over the necklace he'd gifted me only moments ago. "Just like you."

I blush under his praise, heat flooding my cheeks. There's something about Sawyer Blackwood that makes me feel seen—desired—in a way I've never known before.

"Do you trust me, Nora?" He asks suddenly, eyes locked on mine as we stand in the middle of his bedroom—me naked and him half-dressed.

I swallow hard at his serious tone but nod fervently. "Yes."

"Good," he murmurs, pressing a soft kiss to my lips before slowly guiding me backwards onto his bed.

Clothes are shed with haste until we're both bared to each other—a sight that sends blood rushing south in Sawyer's body as he gazes at me with hungry eyes. But there's more than just lust there—I can see it in his gaze—the care and the protectiveness that makes my heart flutter.

"Are you ready?" He asks as he settles himself between my thighs—a sight so erotic I can hardly stand it. I nod, unable to form words in my throat as anticipation swells within me.

His eyes never leave mine as he moves, slowly, steadily. He pushes inside of me with a cautious ease that has me gasping for air. The feeling of him—big and hard—stretching me is intoxicating.

"Holy shit," he mutters, his head falling onto my shoulder as he grunts out his pleasure.

I laugh breathlessly, wrapping my legs around his waist to draw him closer.

"God, Nora...I want to give you everything, baby. You want anything, you just ask me, you hear me?" he pants against my neck, his hot breath sending shivers down my spine.

His thrusts are gentle at first, but soon increase in tempo as he finds his rhythm. I cling to him, nails digging into his broad shoulders as a wave of pleasure washes over me.

"Say my name," he growls into my ear, his voice rough with need and possession. It's a demand, one I'm only too happy to fulfill.

"Sawyer," I moan out, arching my back against him as he drives into me with a powerful thrust.

He makes love to me like a man starved—hungry, desperate and filled with a fiery intensity that leaves me dizzy. His kisses are fervent and his touch demanding, staking a claim on my body that leaves no room for doubt—I am his and he is mine.

My heart races as Sawyer's lips trail down my neck, teasingly nipping and sucking at my skin. His strong hands grip my hips fiercely, urging me to meet his passionate kisses with the same fervor. He groans against my lips, sending shivers of desire coursing through my veins.

"Sawyer," I pant, my voice trembling with anticipation. He peppers soft bites along my jawline before capturing my bottom lip between his teeth and tugging gently. A moan escapes me as he does so, echoing his hungry growl.

His hand moves to cup my breast through my dress, squeezing gently, and then roughly pinching my nipple. I arch my back involuntarily, my breath catching. He grinds his hips against me, rubbing his erection against my clit, driving me wild.

"You were made for me, little girl. You know that? And I'm going to take care of you forever. You're mine," he whispers in my ear, his voice thick with lust. It sends a wave of heat coursing through my body, making me wetter for him.

He pulls back slightly, his gaze holding mine captive as he runs a finger over my swollen lips. Then, without warning, he thrusts two fingers deep inside me, filling me up and claiming me as his own.

"Fuck," he groans, watching my face contort in pleasure. "You love this, don't you?" His voice is rough and demanding, but there's a hint of vulnerability there too.

"Yes," I moan, my body begging for more. I can feel myself growing wetter for him with each passing second.

He releases my nipple, only to wrap his hand around my throat and pull me closer. I gasp, feeling a flood of emotions rush through me. This is exactly what I want—to be taken, possessed, and owned by him.

"Do you want me to fuck you?" he asks, his voice low and menacing. I nod frantically, my eyes never leaving his. "Say it."

"Please, Sawyer," I whisper, my heart racing in anticipation. "Fuck me hard."

He grins wickedly at that, his eyes glinting with a dangerous promise. "As you wish, darlin'." Without any further delay, he aligns himself with my entrance and pushes in swiftly. The sudden intrusion has me gasping in surprise and pleasure.

"Shit, Nora," he hisses through clenched teeth as he starts to move. His thrusts are rough and possessive, matching the demanding tone of his voice from earlier. It's all so intoxicating—the feel of him inside me, the lust in his eyes, the sound of our bodies slapping together in a frantic rhythm.

His fingers dig into my hips as he sets a brutal pace, driving into me over and over again. The room fills with the sounds of our desperate moans and heavy breaths.

"I want to hear you scream my name," Sawyer growls, leaning down to capture my mouth in a searing kiss. His tongue explores my mouth with the same fervor he's displaying physically.

A low moan escapes my lips as he thrusts even harder, hitting that sweet spot inside me that has my vision blurring from pleasure. He growls in response, nipping at my bottom lip before pulling away to gaze down at me with lust-filled eyes.

"You're so damn wet for me," he pants out, sounding shocked and pleased at the same time.

The rawness in his voice is enough to push me over the edge. My climax hits me like a freight train, leaving me writhing and gasping beneath him as wave after wave of pleasure crashes over me.

"Sawyer!"

"Yes, that's in, darlin'. Come on your man's big dick. Let me feel it, baby."

His words, as rough and coarse as they are, act as a catalyst. My climax rushes over me, leaving me in a state of dazed euphoria. I moan his name over and over again, my voice echoing through the room.

"Fucking hell," he groans, his pace quickening as he chases his own release. Grunts and heavy breaths mix with our desperate moans.

My body tightens around him as I ride out my orgasm, the sensation sending tremors down Sawyer's spine. His grip on my hips tightens to the brink of pain, grounding me in this moment—in this deliciously raw tangle of limbs and whispered confessions.

"Fuck, baby," he pants against my neck, shuddering as he buries himself deep within me one last time. I can feel the warmth of his release filling me up, marking me as his in a way no one else can ever hope to.

As he collapses onto me, chest heaving with exertion and satisfaction, I can't help but wrap my arms around him. He's mine just as much as I am his—a fact that neither of us can deny now.

"I need you." He murmurs against my shoulder, pressing soft kisses to my skin. "I don't want anyone else to touch you."

His possessive words send shivers down my spine even after the haze of our climax has faded away. There's a sense of rightness to it all, like this is where I'm supposed to be, wrapped up in his arms and claimed by his touch.

My fingers trace the hard lines of his muscular back. His possessiveness sends a thrill of anticipation through my veins. I want him in every possible way, just as much as he wants me. "I'm all yours."

He lifts his head to look at me, his deep blue eyes filled with a multitude of emotions—lust and love, possession and vulnerability. His hand comes up to gently caress my face, his thumb brushing over my bottom lip in a barely-there touch that sends shivers down my spine.

"Swear it," he demands, his voice rough yet filled with a desperate need that tugs at my heartstrings. He wants reassurance, confirmation that I belong to him as much as he belongs to me.

"I swear," I promise him earnestly, meeting his gaze without any hesitation. "I'm yours, Sawyer. Only yours."

That seems to satisfy him because he grins down at me before leaning in to kiss me deeply. His tongue slips past my lips, exploring my mouth with a fervor that leaves no room for doubt—I am his and he is mine.

CHAPTER
FIVE

Sawyer

THE BARN DOOR SLAMS OPEN, nearly coming off its hinges, and there stands Edward Davenport. His face? Red like the devil's backside after a trip down a steep slide. He marches straight up to me, that vein in his forehead looking like it's about to pop.

"End it with Nora!" he barks, spitting fire with each word. "You've taken enough from her innocence, Blackwood."

I'm on my feet in a heartbeat, every muscle tensed, ready for whatever this storm's gonna throw at me. "Listen, Ed," I start, my voice low and steady, "I ain't taking advantage of nobody. Nora? She's something special, and I care about her. More than you know."

"Care?" Edward snorts, throwing the word out like it's a curse. "Is that what you call leaving hickeys on her neck? That girl is barely out of high school, and you're—what?—some big-shot rancher who thinks he can have whatever he wants?"

"Damn right I'm a rancher," I shoot back, stepping closer, feeling the heat from his anger and the chill from mine collide. "And I want Nora. But not like some prize, not like you're thinking. I want her heart, not just her body, though, hell, I'd be lying if I said I didn't want that too."

"Her heart?" he scoffs, shaking his head like I'm selling him swamp land in the desert. "You think love is marked by bruises on her skin?"

"Love is a lot of things," I say, my jaw so clenched it might crack. "It's messy, it's raw, and yeah, sometimes it leaves a mark. But it's real, Ed. What Nora and I have? It's as real as the dirt under our boots."

"Real or not, you'll end it, or I swear to God—"

"Or what?" I cut him off, my eyes blazing now. "You'll take her away? Tell her she can't make her own choices? She's eighteen, Ed. And she chose me."

"Because you've blinded her with your... your..."

"Come on, Ed," I interrupt him, "let's not pretend

this isn't killing you because she's your little girl. I get it. But don't make her pay for your fears."

"Pay for—you think you're some kind of gift to her?"

"Hell, I'm no gift," I concede, my tone softening just a notch. "But I'm someone who'll fight for her, stand by her, and give her all of me. Can you honestly tell her she shouldn't have that?"

His fists clench and unclench at his sides, and I know I've hit a nerve. Maybe because deep down, he knows it too. Love ain't clean-cut and pretty like in those romance novels. It's gritty, it's hard, and yeah, sometimes it leaves you breathless and wanting more.

The barn door bangs open, and Nora bursts in, her breath coming fast. Her eyes are wide—like she's just seen a ghost in broad daylight. I can tell from the way she's looking at me, at her dad, that she's swimming in shock, trying to grasp what's unfolding in front of her.

"Da-Dad?" Her voice shakes as much as her hands. She's caught between the fury in her old man's eyes and the stubborn set of my jaw, a deer trapped in the headlights of a slow-motion collision.

"Sweetheart," Edward's tone flips like a switch, all soft and pleading now, all that anger he had aimed at me turning into something like fear, "you gotta end this with Sawyer. For your own good."

He steps closer to her, reaching out but not quite

touching—as if he's afraid she'll flinch away or break down. And damn, it slices through me to see her so lost, her father so desperate.

"Please, baby girl." His eyes are pools of worry, dark with the thought of her getting hurt. "I've seen things, been around long enough to know how the world works. He's older, experienced, and you...you're just starting out."

"Edward..." I bite back the urge to argue, to defend myself against his words, because this ain't about him and me right now—it's about Nora. It's always been about her.

"Look at me, Nora." Edward's got that edge of urgency creeping into his voice, like he's hanging onto reason by a thread. "You think you love him, but it's a big world out there. You don't need to get tied down to the first man who shows you attention."

But hell, I know it's more than attention between me and Nora. It's a fire that can't be doused by doubt or fear, not by mine nor her daddy's. It's raw and real, and it kills me that I can't shout that truth for both of them to hear.

Nora bites her lip.

Damn.

I can't stand here and watch her crumble under the weight of her father's fears. I step forward, my boots thudding on the worn wooden floor of the barn.

"Nora," I start, my voice low but unwavering, "I know this is hard, and I know your daddy's only lookin' out for you, but what we have..." My hand reaches out to her, hovering in the space between us, desperate to bridge it. "It's real, darlin'. Don't let fear steal away something that could be damn beautiful."

Her eyes, those big doe-like pools reflecting a storm of emotions, meet mine. Tears brim and threaten to spill over, carving wet trails down her cheeks. She blinks rapidly, trying to hold them back, trying to hold everything back.

"Your dad's right about one thing—I am experienced," I admit, and there's no shame in that truth because with every year, every heartbreak, I've built up to this moment, to her. "But that just means I know when something's worth fightin' for. And Nora, you're worth every damn second of the fight."

She stands frozen, a statue carved of confusion and longing, torn between the pull of her blood and the call of her heart. Her lips part slightly, trembling as if they're battling the words that want to escape.

"Dad says..." Her voice is barely above a whisper, carried away by the tension in the room. "Sawyer, I don't know if I can—"

"Can what?" I push gently, needing her to voice it, to own whatever fear's got her shackled. "Can stand up for yourself? Can choose who to love? 'Cause I think you can, Nora. You're strong, fierce even. Don't let anyone, not even him," I nod toward Edward, my gaze never leaving hers, "tell you otherwise."

The silence stretches between us, so thick I reckon I could lasso it. She chews on her bottom lip—a nervous habit I've come to find endearing—and I see the battle raging within her. Love versus loyalty. Desire versus duty. It's tearing her apart, and fuck if it doesn't tear at me too.

"Say something, darlin'," I coax, willing her to speak her mind, to listen to that wild heart I know beats inside her chest. "Tell me you feel it too. This ain't just some fling. It's you and me, against the odds."

Nora's shoulders slump as if the burden's grown too heavy. Her tears finally break free, rushing down her face like a river after a storm. Yet, despite the downpour, there's a fire in her eyes that refuses to be snuffed out.

"Sawyer, I—" She starts, but the rest gets lost, choked back by a sob.

"Take your time," I say softly, giving her the space she needs because I know this ain't easy. But I also know we won't get nowhere if we don't face this head-on, together. The rawness, the intensity of it all—it's what makes this real. It's what makes *us* real.

The air in the barn's thick with tension, a storm brewing in Edward's eyes—a hurricane about to make landfall on my damn face. His step forward is all it takes, and his fist comes swinging like a sledgehammer. I don't back down, never have, not with the stakes this high.

"Damn it, Sawyer! Stay away from my daughter!" Edward snarls, a wild fire in his gaze.

"Like hell I will," I grunt out as I dodge his punch, feeling the whoosh of air as it narrowly misses my jaw. I ain't no stranger to a brawl, but fighting Nora's father? That's a new level of hell I hadn't planned on visiting.

"Stop it! Both of you, please!" Nora's scream slices through the cacophony of our grunts and the thud of fists against flesh.

I throw a punch that lands square on Edward's shoulder, feeling the jolt run up my arm. He retaliates with a blow that grazes my cheek. We're two rams butting heads, locked in a battle neither is willing to lose. Every hit, every grunt echoes Nora's name in my head—she's the reason for this fight, the prize, and the damn referee all rolled into one.

Nora rushes toward us, her hands reaching out in a futile attempt at peacekeeping. "Dad! Sawyer! Please, this isn't the way!"

"Stay out of it, Nora!" Edward roars, even as he throws another punch, which I sidestep, my boots scuffing the dirt floor.

"Fuck, Eddie, don't you see you're scaring her?" I spit out between clenched teeth, trying to keep my focus, though every cell in my body screams to wrap Nora up and shield her from this ugliness.

"Scaring her? You're corrupting her, you son of a—" His words cut off with a grunt as I land a solid hit, and I'm not sure if it's satisfaction or regret that twists in my gut.

"Stop hurting each other!" Nora's plea's desperate, her voice shattering against the wooden beams above.

Her face is a canvas of fear and anguish, tears streaking down her cheeks, and it stabs at me sharper than any punch ever could. This ain't what I wanted— for her to witness her world, her men, her heart, clashing in a violent dance meant for enemies, not lovers, not family.

"Enough!" The word explodes from her lips, and everything freezes for a heartbeat—my fist midair, Edward's face a mask of rage, the dust swirling around us like specters.

A sob breaks from her chest, raw and ragged, slicing through the chaos. It's the sound of breaking— her heart, my resolve, the very earth beneath our feet.

"Please," she whimpers, and God, if that plea doesn't bring me to my knees.

I shove Edward hard, and he stumbles back. Blood tastes like iron in my mouth, and I swipe at the trickle leaking from my split lip. My chest rises and falls like I've been running miles instead of trading blows with a man old enough to know better. But hell, I should've known better too.

"Look what you've done!" Nora cries out, her voice trembling worse than a leaf in a storm.

Her eyes—those big, soulful ones that hooked me from day one—are wide with shock and glistening with unshed tears. It's like looking into a mirror that reflects all my screw-ups, and it hits me square in the chest. I may have just lost her.

"Baby, I—" I start, but words are damn useless now.

She doesn't wait for me to stitch together some apology. With a heart-wrenching sob, she turns on her heel, a blur of sun-kissed hair and raw emotion, tearing out the barn door faster than a spooked colt. Her small figure gets swallowed up by the sprawling ranch outside, leaving nothing but dust devils dancing in her wake.

"Damn it, Edward," I growl, glaring at him through the haze of pain and regret. "You pushed her to this."

"Me?" He's panting, disbelief etched across his aging features. "You're the one who—"

"Enough!" I cut him off because if I hear one more word, I might just take a swing at my own reflection next.

The barn feels hauntingly empty without Nora's

presence, her absence a void no amount of anger can fill. I'm left standing there, my fists still balled at my sides, the taste of blood and fear thick on my tongue. The silence throbs louder than any punch ever could, and I can't shake the feeling that I've messed up in ways that can't be punched or kissed away.

"Shit." I whisper, the word as broken as the scene before me.

I've got to go after her. She could get hurt. She's in no right mind to be running off on her own.

I burst out the barn door, boots kicking up dust and heart hammering against my ribs like it's trying to break free. Panic is a wildfire in my veins, burning me up as I scan the sprawling ranch for any sign of her.

"Fuck, fuck, fuck," I mutter under my breath, every curse a prayer that she hasn't gone far. The horizon stretches out, taunting me with its vastness, hiding Nora somewhere in its golden waves.

"Noraaa!" My voice rips from my throat, raw and desperate. It echoes back at me, empty and unanswered. She could be anywhere, hidden by the rolling hills or tucked away in one of the countless nooks on Blackwood land.

I sprint past the stables, my eyes flicking over each fence and thicket, searching for that familiar glint of sunlit hair, aching for a glimpse of her lithe frame. I know every inch of this goddamn property, but right now it feels like foreign territory, every second without her stretching into an eternity.

As I round the bend near the old oak grove, my breath hitches. There's a spot there, a secret place tangled with wildflowers and shaded by ancient branches, where I once caught Nora staring out at the sunset, her face awash with peace. It calls to me now, whispering promises of refuge and solace.

My jog slows to a walk as I approach, every step filled with dread and hope fighting for dominance. Then I see her, a small figure crumpled at the base of an oak tree, her body shaking with sobs that cut through the still air.

"Ah, hell, Nora." The sight of her, so broken and alone, tears at something inside me, fierce and sharp. Her vulnerability, laid bare among the wildflowers, is a punch straight to the gut.

She doesn't notice me at first, too lost in her own world of hurt. I crouch down beside her, close enough to reach out but too shaken to touch. Her sobs are a gut-wrenching melody, and every tear that falls is an accusation, a reminder of the chaos I've caused.

"Shit, Nora," I mutter under my breath as relief floods through me, so potent it's damn near crippling. I can't lose her, won't let that happen.

She's a sight, all vulnerability and raw beauty, and it hits me hard in the chest. My girl, out here alone, because of me. My determination kicks in, fierce as a prairie fire. I'm gonna fix this, make everything right for her.

"Hey," I call out softly, not wanting to startle her more than she already is.

Nora's head snaps up, and our eyes lock. Hers are swimming with tears, making my heart lurch painfully. But there's more—pain mixed with something that looks a heck of a lot like longing. It's a punch in the gut, that look. She's torn up inside, just like me.

I take a hesitant step forward, my hand outstretched like I'm trying to catch a spooked mare. "Nora, listen to me, please."

She's looking at me, really looking, and it's like she can see straight into the mess that's my heart. The place where her name is carved deep.

"Every moment you're near, it's like I'm alive for the first time." My voice shakes, betraying the storm inside me. "It's raw and real, and damn it, Nora, I know I've screwed up, but I can't—won't—let you walk away from what we have."

Her eyes flit to my hand, still hanging in the air between us, and something flickers there. Hope? Fear? Both are so tangled up in us it's hard to tell.

"Your dad thinks I'm just some rough-around-the-edges rancher who's after one thing." I scoff lightly, trying to keep it light even though my insides are coiling tight with angst. "But hell, baby, he doesn't know that you're under my skin, you're in my bones. You're the fire in my blood."

She bites her lip, and I have to hold back a groan. That lip, those eyes—God, they've haunted my dreams more times than I can count.

"Every night," I continue, my hand now shaking so bad I have to lower it before she sees, "I lie awake thinking about you, about us. And yeah, maybe it's crazy fast and all-consuming, but when I touch you, when you look at me like you do...I know it's worth fighting for."

"Is it, Sawyer? Do you…do you love me?" Her voice is small, barely above a whisper, but it cuts through the silence like the sharpest blade.

"More than anything in this world," I admit, dead serious. "Without you, Nora, it's like someone turned off the damn sun."

There's a beat of silence, a single heartbeat where I think she might just walk away and leave me here, broken. But then, she steps closer, and I dare to breathe again.

"Make me believe it, Sawyer. Make me feel it."

And I don't need to be told twice. I close the distance, my hands finding her waist, and I pull her against me. My lips crash onto hers, pouring every ounce of regret, longing, and plain old desire into that kiss. I kiss her like it's the first time and the last time all at once, like I'm a man dying of thirst and she's the only well for miles.

"Believe me now?" I murmur against her lips, almost afraid to let her go long enough to hear her answer.

"Convince me more," she breathes, and damn if that isn't the best invitation I've ever had.

With my lips still pressed against hers, I slide my hands up her back and into her hair, pulling her closer. She moans into the kiss, and I can taste her desire on my tongue. My cock throbs in agreement, begging to be freed from its confinement. As we break apart for air, I gaze down at her flushed cheeks and hungry eyes.

"Do you see what you do to me?" I growl, my voice rough with lust. "You're the only one who can make me lose control like this."

She bites her bottom lip, eyeing me with a mixture of curiosity and nervousness. "I want you to take control," she pants. "Show me what you've got."

I nod, my mind reeling with possibilities. I slowly begin to undo the buttons on her shirt, my fingers tracing the skin beneath as I expose more of her. I toss her shirt aside and trail my fingers down the center of her chest, teasing the edges of her bra. I grab the sides of her bra and yank it down, freeing her perfect breasts.

She gasps as they're exposed to the cool air, her nipples already hardened from my touch. I reach out and pinch one between my thumb and forefinger, eliciting a soft moan from her lips.

"You like that?" I ask, leaning in to suckle on her nipple while twisting the other between my fingers.

"Oh god yes," she whimpers, arching her back in pleasure.

I trail my lips down her stomach, over her bellybutton, and further south until I reach the hem of her skirt. With a quick tug, it's off and thrown aside. My eyes feast on the sight of her little pink panties, barely containing her wetness. I kneel down before her, taking one of her legs in my hand and spreading her open.

"Now let me show you what I've got," I whisper, running my tongue along the edge of her panties.

She gasps, her fingers digging into my shoulders as I tease her. Without further ado, I press my tongue against her folds, tasting her sweetness. She tastes even better than I remember. As I continue to lick and suckle her, my other hand reaches down to rub her clit, sending shockwaves of pleasure through her body.

"Please," she begs, her voice hoarse. "Fuck me."

I smile against her pussy and then settle atop her int he grass, my leaking cock nudging against her wet hole.

"I would do anything for you, darlin'. You gotta know that," I tell her as I push into her.

She whimpers, her eyes never leaving mine as I continue pushing into her until I'm seated all the way inside her hot heat, my balls resting against her ass.

Fuuuck, she feels so good.

"I love you too," she finally says. "I want to be with you forever, Sawyer."

And that's all I need to hear to make me lose it.

I smash my lips onto hers and fuck into her like a madman.

Mine! Mine! Mine!

"Sawyer!" She's screaming my name in no time, and when I feel her little pussy fluttering around me, it's all I need to make me come harder than I've ever come in my entire life.

We lay there in the grass, my girl cradled against my chest, both of us still shaking in the aftermath of our orgasms.

"No one's ever going to take you away from me," I vow.

She snuggles closer to my chest, and I stroke her hair. "Good," she says.

My Nora.

EPILOGUE

One year later

Nora

I STAND NEXT TO SAWYER, the expanse of our ranch stretching out before us like a promise kept, bathed in the golden kisses of the setting sun. His presence is as solid and reassuring as the earth under my boots, the quiet strength of him seeping into me, filling every nook and cranny with warmth and an undeniable sense of home.

"Beautiful, isn't it?" I murmur, unable to tear my gaze from the horizon where the sun flirts with the edge of the world, turning the sky into a canvas splashed with fiery reds and soft purples.

"Nothing compared to you," he says, his voice a low rumble that tickles my spine in all the right ways. His eyes aren't on the sunset. They're on me, filled with that smoldering intensity that always sets my blood on fire.

Sawyer's fingers lace with mine, strong and sure, and we start walking, our steps in sync. Each echo of our boots against the earth whispers secrets of our shared path, the ups and downs, the passion and the tenderness. The sort of journey that romance novels try to capture but never quite get right—because this, us, it's realer than any paperback fantasy.

We head towards that secret spot of ours, the one that's etched into my memory and branded onto my skin. The place where I first surrendered to the wild rhythm of his desires, where I learned what it meant to be truly wanted, to be cherished and claimed in the same heartbeat.

"Remember that night?" he asks, a devilish grin tugging at his lips. It's like he's read my mind or maybe it's just that we're so attuned to each other now, our thoughts run parallel lines that inevitably cross at every important moment.

"Hard to forget," I shoot back, playful sass in my tone. "You, me, the stars as our only witness." My heart thumps louder, remembering the raw urgency of our coming together, the way he looked at me like I was the first and last woman on Earth.

"Best damn night of my life," he declares, his thumb caressing the back of my hand, sending little zings of anticipation dancing up my arm.

"Mine too," I admit, because it's true. With Sawyer, every touch is a spark, every glance a promise of more —more heat, more laughter, more love. And I can't help but feel lucky, like I've hit the jackpot in the lottery of love.

Sawyer's arms envelop me, his rugged strength a fortress as we reach our secret hideaway. The world falls away, leaving just the two of us in this slice of paradise where it all began. His hands are firm and sure on my back, pulling me closer until I'm pressed against the solid wall of his chest. My skin tingles where he touches, sparks of electricity that weave their way down my spine.

"Hey there, darlin'," he murmurs, his breath warm against my ear before his lips capture mine. It's a kiss that speaks of sun-soaked days and starlit nights, of a love as vast as the Texas sky above us. I melt into him, giving as good as I get, our tongues dancing a familiar dance that never gets old.

"God, Sawyer..." I gasp when we finally break apart, my voice thick with desire and something deeper, something that's grown every day since I said 'I do.' I look up into his eyes—those deep pools of midnight—and find myself drowning in the intensity I see there. "Do you have any idea how much I love being your wife?"

His smile is slow, filled with the knowledge of just how well he's loved me, every inch, every curve. "Tell me anyway," he says, that competitive glint I know so well flashing across his gaze.

"More than the stars love the night sky," I whisper fiercely. "You've lit up my life in ways I didn't even know were dark. You've given me a world where I am wanted, cherished... adored." My hands roam over the hard planes of his body, feeling the ripple of muscles beneath my fingertips. "Being with you, it's like...it's like I've been thirsty my whole life and you're my tall drink of water."

"Damn, Nora." His voice is low, rough with emotion. "You make it sound like some kind of fairytale."

"Isn't it?" I challenge, tilting my head back to catch his gaze. "You're my knight in shining cowboy boots."

He laughs then, a rich sound that echoes in the quiet around us. "And you're my badass princess. The Bonnie to my Clyde."

"Without the crime spree," I add quickly, and we both chuckle, lost in our own perfect little world.

"Without the crime spree," he agrees, sealing the vow with another kiss, one that promises an eternity of passion and partnership. And I think to myself, hell yes, this is my fairytale, and I'm living it every single day.

The sun dips lower, streaking the sky with ribbons of pink and orange, as Sawyer leans in close, his breath warm against the shell of my ear. "Nora, honey," he murmurs, and the shivers that dance down my spine have nothing to do with the evening chill. "I swear on this land—on everything I am—I'll protect you." His voice is a heady mix of promise and raw desire.

"Protect me from what?" I tease, tilting my head to look at him, but my heart's racing because I know he means every word.

"From anything that dares to mess with my woman," he says, his gaze fierce, like he could take on the world for me. And just like that, my knees go weak because damn it, that's exactly what I want.

"Your woman, huh?" I play along, biting my lip as I let my hands start to wander, tracing the hard lines of his chest through his shirt. "What makes you think I need protecting?"

"Because you're precious, more than you know," he whispers, his hands finding the hem of my shirt. "And I'm not about to let anything tarnish that."

There's this heat in his eyes, a spark that tells me

he's not all talk. It's the same spark that lit the fire between us, the one that's been burning ever since. We're alone out here, surrounded by nothing but open space and the fading light, and I can't help but think there's no place I'd rather be.

"Show me then," I dare him, my voice dropping to a huskier tone. "Protect me, cherish me..."

Sawyer doesn't need telling twice. He pulls my shirt over my head, his fingers skimming along my skin with a reverence that sends my heart into a tailspin. My own hands aren't idle. They're busy working the buttons of his shirt, popping them open one by one with an eagerness that's mirrored in his darkening eyes.

"God, Nora, you're beautiful," he breathes out as my shirt lands somewhere in the grass, forgotten.

"Right back atcha, cowboy," I shoot back with a grin, pushing his shirt off his shoulders. It's like unwrapping a present I've been dying to get my hands on all day. The sight of his tanned, muscled torso under the twilight sky—it's enough to make a girl believe in magic.

His hands are on me again, sliding my jeans down my hips with a slowness that's pure torture. Every inch of skin revealed is worshiped with his touch, with his lips following closely behind, setting every nerve ending on fire.

"Seems only fair," I murmur, reaching for his belt buckle with nimble fingers. It's not just about getting naked. It's a dance we're doing, a slow burn that's about to ignite into something wild.

"Fair's my middle name," he growls, but there's a playful glint in his eyes that tells me he's enjoying this as much as I am.

Our clothes become a memory, discarded carelessly around us as we stand there in the dying light, skin to skin. There's urgency there, sure, but it's tempered with something deeper, something sacred. We're baring more than our bodies—we're baring our souls, and as our skin meets, it feels like coming home.

We collapse onto the grass, a blanket of stars above us, our breaths mingling in the crisp night air. Sawyer's chest is a solid wall against my back as he pulls me closer, his arms a vise locking me in a cocoon of warmth and security. I tilt my head to catch his lips with mine, and we kiss—a deep, soul-stirring melding that speaks volumes more than words ever could.

"God, Nora," he whispers against my mouth, his voice husky with desire. "I can't get enough of you."

"Then don't," I challenge, arching into him with a playful smirk. "Keep going."

His hands are everywhere, tracing the contours of my body with an artist's precision, mapping out the territory he claims as his own. The touch of his fingers ignites a blazing trail of heat wherever they roam—down the dip of my waist, over the rise of my hips, along the length of my thighs. I'm alive under his touch, every cell buzzing with anticipation, craving more of his attention.

"Tell me what you want, sweetheart," Sawyer's voice rumbles low in my ear, sending shivers down my spine.

"Everything," I gasp out, breathless. "Give me everything."

And he does. His movements sync with mine in a rhythm as old as time, pushing and pulling, giving and taking. It's a dance we've perfected, bodies and hearts entwined, moving together toward the same inevitable climax. There's a ferocity in the way he loves me, a raw passion that leaves no room for anything but the moment we're lost in.

Above us, the sky is a canvas of darkness dotted with twinkling lights, each star a silent witness to the fervor of our union. As we build higher, there's nothing left but Sawyer and me—the only two people who have ever existed.

"Look at the stars, Nora," he breathes out, his voice strained with the effort to remain coherent. "They're shining just for you."

"Only because you're with me." My reply is a whisper, a secret meant only for him.

Our cries rise up to those stars as we find our release, a cry that blends seamlessly with the night's quiet serenade. We're wrapped in a bubble of ecstasy, our connection so profound it feels like we've touched the divine.

"Damn, we're good together," I pant, still clinging to him as aftershocks ripple through us.

"The best," he agrees, pressing a kiss to my sweat-dampened forehead.

In the afterglow, we lay tangled in each other, a satisfied tangle of limbs on the cool grass beneath the celestial audience. There's no place I'd rather be than here, in Sawyer's arms, with the promise of forever whispered on the wind.

I roll onto my side, the blades of grass tickling the bare skin of my back, and look at Sawyer. His chest rises and falls with easy breaths, those broad shoulders casting a silhouette against the starry night. We're still wrapped up in each other, literally and figuratively, and I can't help but trace the lines of his jaw with my fingertips.

"Hey," he whispers, a lopsided grin forming on his lips as he catches my hand in his, bringing it to his mouth for a gentle kiss.

"Hey yourself," I shoot back, my voice low and husky. The air is charged with the remnants of our passion, thick with the scent of wildflowers and that musky, deliciously male aroma that is all Sawyer.

"I love you, Nora. More than this land, more than the sky above us," he murmurs, those intense blue eyes locking onto mine.

"Good, 'cause you're stuck with me." My laughter is a soft thing, a bubble of joy that floats up into the night. "I love you too, cowboy."

We stay like that for a while, just talking softly, saying little things that mean so much. Each word is a caress, every sentence a vow. It's not just about the heat between us—which, let's be honest, could start another wildfire—it's about the connection. The bond that tells me I'm his and he's mine.

Eventually, we start to dress, and it's a languid process filled with stolen kisses and lingering touches. I watch him pull on his jeans, that backside of his deserving its own zip code, and I bite my lip to keep from dragging him back down to the ground.

"Ready to head back?" he asks, holding out his hand to help me up.

"Lead the way, Mr. Blackwood." I wink, slipping my feet into my boots and shrugging on my shirt.

As we button up and dust off, our gazes meet, and there's an entire conversation in that silent exchange. Life's gonna throw curveballs, we know that. But together, we've got an arsenal of love to knock them out of the park.

Hand in hand, we make our way back to reality, the stars winking out one by one, like they're closing their eyes on a secret only Sawyer and I share.

Dust kicks up under our boots as Sawyer and I walk hand in hand, the crunch of dry grass beneath us like a rhythm to the melody of crickets serenading the twilight. The ranch sprawls out before us, a kingdom of open fields and endless possibilities.

"Imagine this all lit up for a party," I muse out loud, my heart doing a little skip at the thought. "Lights strung from every post, music floating on the breeze. A dance floor right there, under the stars."

"Only the best for my girl," Sawyer says, his voice deep and velvety in the cooling air. "We'll have the whole county talking about it for years."

I giggle, squeezing his hand. "And then some peace and quiet, just us, maybe a few tiny pairs of feet pattering around?" The future unfurls in my mind like a movie montage, full of laughter and soft gazes, the kind of life that sets your roots deep and your spirit soaring.

"Tiny feet, huh?" He arches a brow, the corners of his mouth quirking up in that mischievous grin that spells trouble—and I'm all for it. "How many are we talking?"

"Enough to start our own little rodeo." I wink at him, and he chuckles, the sound mingling with the sigh of the wind through the trees.

"Sounds perfect, Nora. Anything you want, it's yours. This life is ours to build, brick by brick, dream by dream."

The promise in his words wraps around me, warm and sure as his arms were moments ago. We're painting our future in broad strokes, bold and fearless. It's exciting, a little scary, and utterly, completely ours.

As we draw closer to the house, I notice a lone figure standing off to the side, watching us approach.

Dad.

His eyes are fixed on us, and there's something in his stance that's different—less stiff, more...yielding?

"Hey, look," I nudge Sawyer with my elbow, nodding toward my father. "It's Dad."

Sawyer follows my gaze, his face softening with understanding. "He's giving us his blessing, you know. In his own way."

I can see it now—the tightness around his eyes has relaxed, and his shoulders aren't quite so squared against the world—or against Sawyer. As we get closer, Dad takes a deep breath and steps forward. There's a moment when everything hangs in the balance, a silent standoff between past worries and future hopes.

Then, just like that, he closes the distance, his rough

hands enveloping both of ours. His nod isn't grudging. It's weighted with acceptance. And as he looks at Sawyer—not as the boss or the older man who swept his daughter off her feet, but as the person I love—he offers a simple, heartfelt "Take good care of her."

"Always," Sawyer promises, his grip firm and reassuring.

"Thanks, Dad," I whisper, feeling the last piece of an intricate puzzle click into place. My heart swells, full to bursting with love—for Sawyer, for this land, for the family we'll be, and for the man who raised me to chase after the happiness I've found right here, in cowboy boots and wide-open spaces.

"Come on," Sawyer nudges me gently, and we start toward the porch again. "Let's go home."

Want a free book from Emma Bray? Go to www.authoremmabray.com.